Purple, Green and Yellow

To Brigid Thurgood, Toronto, Ontario — R.M.
To Pénélope Link — H.D.

©1992 Bob Munsch Enterprises Ltd. (text)
©1992 Hélène Desputeaux (art)
Graphic design and realization by Michel Aubin.

Twenty-second printing, December 2005

Annick Press Ltd.

We acknowledge the support of the Canada Council for the Arts, the Ontario
Arts Council, and the Government of Canada through the Book Publishing
Industry Development Program (BPIDP) for our publishing activities.

Cataloging in Publication Data
    Munsch, Robert N., 1945–
      Purple, green and yellow

(Munsch for kids)
ISBN 1-55037-255-6 (bound) ISBN 1-55037-256-4 (pbk.)

I. Desputeaux, Hélène. II. Title. III. Series:
Munsch, Robert N., 1945– Munsch for kids.

PS8576.U57P87 1992 JC813'.54 C92-093878-7
PZ7.M85Pu 1992

The art in this book was rendered in watercolors.
The text was typeset in American Typewriter.

Distributed in Canada by: Published in the U.S.A. by Annick Press (U.S.) Ltd.
Firefly Books Ltd.   Distributed in the U.S.A. by:
66 Leek Crescent   Firefly Books (U.S.) Inc.
Richmond Hill, ON   P.O. Box 1338
L4B 1H1   Ellicott Station
                         Buffalo, NY 14205

Printed and bound in China.

visit us at: **www.annickpress.com**

Purple, Green and Yellow

story by
Robert Munsch

illustrated by
Hélène Desputeaux

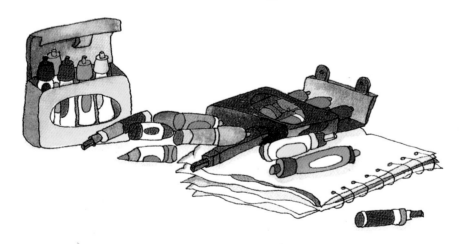

Annick Press Ltd.
Toronto • New York • Vancouver

Brigid went to her mother and said, "I need some coloring markers. All my friends have coloring markers. They draw wonderful pictures. Mommy, I need some coloring markers."

"Oh, no!" said her mother. "I've heard about those coloring markers. Kids draw on walls, they draw on the floor, they draw on themselves. You can't have any coloring markers."

"ell," said Brigid, "there are these new coloring markers. They wash off with just water. I can't get into any trouble with coloring markers that wash off. Get me some of those."

"Well," said her mother, "all right."

So her mother went out and got Brigid 500 washable coloring markers.

Brigid went up to her room and drew wonderful pictures. She drew lemons that were yellower than lemons, and roses that were redder than roses, and oranges that were oranger than oranges.

Her mother was amazed.
She said, "Wow! My kid is an artist."

But after a week Brigid got bored. She went to her mother and said, "Mom, did I draw on the wall?"

"Nnnnooo," said her mother.
"Did I draw on the floor?"
"Nnnnooo," said her mother.
"Did I draw on myself?"
"Nnnnooo," said her mother.

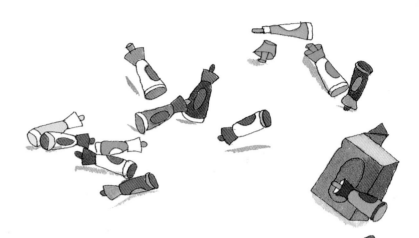

"Well," said Brigid, "I didn't get into any trouble and I need some new coloring markers. All my friends have them. Mommy, there are coloring markers that smell. They have ones that smell like roses and lemons and oranges and even ones that smell like cow plops. Mom, they have coloring markers that smell like anything you want! Mom, I need those coloring markers."

Her mother went out and got 500 coloring markers that smelled. Then Brigid went upstairs and she drew pictures. She drew lemons that smelled like lemons, and roses that smelled like roses, and oranges that smelled like oranges, and cow plops that smelled like cow plops.

 er mother said, "Wow! My kid is an artist."

Βut after a week Brigid got bored. She said, "Mom, did I draw on the floor?"

"Nnnnooo," said her mother.
"Did I draw on the walls?"
"Nnnnooo," said her mother.
"Did I draw on myself?"
"Nnnnooo," said her mother.

"**W**ell," said Brigid, "I need some new coloring markers. These are the best kind. All my friends have them. They are super-indelible-never-come-off-till-you're-dead-and-maybe-even-later coloring markers. Mom, I need them."

So her mother went out and got 500 super-indelible-never-come-off-till-you're-dead-and-maybe-even-later coloring markers. Brigid took them and drew pictures for three weeks. She drew lemons that looked better than lemons, and roses that looked better than roses and oranges that looked better than oranges and sunsets that looked better than sunsets.

Then she got bored.
She said, "I'm tired of
drawing on the paper. But I am
not going to draw on the walls
and I am not going to draw
on the floor and I'm not going
to draw on myself — but every-
body knows it's okay to color
your fingernails. Even my
mother colors her fingernails."

So Brigid took a purple
super-indelible-never-come-off-
till-you're-dead-and-maybe-
even-later coloring marker,
and she colored her thumbnail
bright purple.

And that was so pretty, she colored all her fingernails purple, black and yellow.

And that was so pretty, she colored her hands yellow, green and red.

And that was so pretty,
she colored her face purple,
green, yellow and blue.

And that was so pretty,
she colored her belly-button
blue.

And that was so pretty, she colored herself all sorts of colors almost entirely all over.

Then Brigid looked in the mirror and said, "What have I done! My mother is going to kill me." So she ran into the bathroom and washed her hands for half an hour. Nothing came off. Her hands still looked like mixed-up rainbows.

Then she had a wonderful idea.

She reached way down into the bottom of the coloring markers and got a special-colored marker. It was the same color she was. She took that marker and colored herself all over until she was her regular color again. In fact, she looked even better than before — almost too good to be true.

She went downstairs and her mother said, "Why, Brigid, you're looking really good today."

"Right," said Brigid.

Then her mother said, "It's time to wash your hands for dinner."

But Brigid was afraid that the special color would not stick to the colors underneath, so she said, "I already washed my hands."

But her mother smelled her hands and said, "Ahhh. No soap!" She took Brigid into the bathroom and washed her hands and face. All the special color came off and Brigid looked like mixed-up rainbows.

"Oh, no!" said her mother. "Brigid, did you color your hands with the coloring markers that wash off?"

"Nnnnooo."

"Brigid, did you color your hands with the coloring markers that smell?"

"Nnnnnooooo."

"Did you use the super-indelible-never-come-off-till-you're-dead-and-maybe-even-later coloring markers?"

"Yes!"

"Yikes!" yelled her mother.

She called the doctor and said, "HELP! HELP! HELP! My daughter has colored herself with super-indelible-never-come-off-till-you're-dead-and-maybe-even-later coloring markers."

"Oh, dear," said the doctor. "Sometimes they never come off."

The doctor came over and gave Brigid a large, orange pill. She said, "Take this pill, wait five minutes and then take a bath."

So Brigid took the pill, waited five minutes, and jumped into the bathtub. Her mother stood outside the door and yelled, "Is it working? Is it working?"

"Yes," said Brigid. "Everything is coming off."
And Brigid was right, everything had come off.
When Brigid walked out of the bathroom she was
invisible.

"Oh, no," yelled her mother. "You can't go to
school if you're invisible. You can't go to university
if you're invisible. You'll never get a job if you're
invisible. Brigid, you've wrecked your life!"

"**D**on't worry," said Brigid. She ran into her room, got the special-colored marker and colored herself entirely all over until you couldn't tell the difference. In fact, she looked even better than before — almost too good to be true.

But her mother said, "Brigid, you can't go through life like that. You're just a picture. Everyone will know there is something wrong."

"No they won't," said Brigid.

"Yes they will," said her mother.

"No they won't," said Brigid. "I colored Daddy while he was taking a nap and you haven't noticed anything yet!"

"Good heavens!" yelled her mother, and she ran into the living room and looked at Daddy. He looked even better than before — almost too good to be true.

"Doesn't he look great?" asked Brigid.

"I couldn't even tell the difference," said her mother.

"Right," said Brigid, "and neither will he...

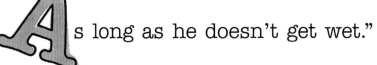

As long as he doesn't get wet."